More Critical Praise for George Pelecanos

for *The Man Who Came Uptown*

"Like his hero Elmore Leonard, Pelecanos finds the humanity in the lowest of lowlifes . . . Pelecanos's peppery dialogue energizes every page." —*Chicago Tribune*

"This is a book about love of family, about the stresses that can lure almost anyone into crime, and about how hard it can be for someone [to] make it on the outside. But most of all, it is a book about the transformative powers of friendship and reading. The story is told in tight, soulful prose by a novelist who has devoted many hours to inmate literacy programs in DC."
—Associated Press

"If I were in jail, George Pelecanos would be on my reading list, right up there with James Lee Burke and Elmore Leonard . . . Pelecanos's characters [are] so human and so doomed. This is an author who writes with the steady hand of a man who knows he's driving a cool set of wheels and respects his own mechanical skills." —*New York Times Book Review*

"A modern storytelling master's paean to the power of books, literature, librarians, and booksellers." —NPR.org

"One of the top ten crime novels of the decade . . . George Pelecanos's tales of tough times in Washington, DC, have all the force, and none of the nonsense, of ancient Greek tragedy."
—*Times* [UK]

"Read this crime novel for entertainment, a look into the human condition in extraordinary circumstances, and for the dissection of the democratic act of the experience of reading great books."
—KUMW

T0038021

"The thriller plot is taut and suspenseful, as jolting as it is carefully nuanced, but it is Pelecanos's focus on character, on his ability to show the richness and depth of his people, as well as their often-heartbreaking yearning for something more, that gives this novel—and all his work—its special power."

—*Booklist*, Starred Review

"Using his customary knowing dialogue and stripped-down, soulful prose, Pelecanos skillfully, sensitively works the urban frontier where the problems and stresses of everyday life cross the line into the sort of criminal behavior that could tempt anyone—anyone at all."

—*Kirkus Reviews*

for *The Double*

"It's astonishing all the good stuff Pelecanos can pack into one unpretentious book that make the story so rich."

—*New York Times Book Review*

"Pungent, funny dialogue . . . believable Black-and-White friendships . . . outstanding scene-setting . . . *The Double* is fast-paced, its villains feel fresh . . . Call me a hard-core Pelecanos junkie."

—*USA Today*

"The author laces his story with vivid descriptions of Washington's changing urban landscape. The writing is taut, the violence is graphic, and the characters are so well-drawn that they step off the page and into your life. *The Double* is as good as it gets."

—Associated Press

for *The Cut*

"The writing is spare; the dialogue rings with authenticity; and walking DC's mean streets with Lucas is the next best thing to being there. Easily the best crime novel I've read this year."

—*Boston Globe*

for *Soul Circus*

"Reading [Pelecanos's novels] makes you realize how contemporary novels are obsessed with the concerns of the middle class and how the poor have been marginalized and reduced to cliché . . . He writes with insight and anger about why young men are drawn into gangs and violent crime . . . Pelecanos understands the lure of violence, the need for action. *Soul Circus* packs a powerful anti-gun message but he can still communicate the thrill of holding a weapon in your hand."   —*New York Times Book Review*

"With each novel, Pelecanos has become more sophisticated . . . It's full of tension and character and it makes you think. It's hard to ask for more than that."   —*Mirror* [UK]

"The twelfth novel by George Pelecanos firmly establishes him as a prince of crime writers who may one day become king."
     —*Esquire*

"Pelecanos has a mean ear for dialogue and a way of propelling the action through speech that's reminiscent of George V. Higgins. His exploration of conflicting moral dilemmas, coupled with a refusal to make his villains all bad and his heroes all good, makes Pelecanos one of America's finest contemporary writers."
     —*Time Out*

for *Right As Rain*

"Glistens with the grit of DC's mean streets."   —*USA Today*

"Slangy, hip . . . one of the very best young mystery writers . . . Pelecanos is the spikiest, stylewise, and probably the most menacing."   —*Esquire*

"One of the best."   —Dennis Lehane

BUSTER
A DOG

GEORGE PELECANOS

BROOKLYN, NEW YORK

Published by Akashic Books
©2024 George Pelecanos
All rights reserved

ISBN: 978-1-63614-170-1
Library of Congress Control Number: 2023949475
First printing

Akashic Books
Brooklyn, New York
Instagram, X/Twitter, Facebook: AkashicBooks
info@akashicbooks.com
www.akashicbooks.com

To Rosa

MISS DARCIA

I f you are like me, the memories of your early days in
this world are sometimes vivid, while others are difficult to recall. I remember playing and roughhousing
with my brothers and sisters, but I can only bring back
one sibling, a girl named Sandy, clearly in my mind. I see
a leopard-print squeeze toy, shaped like a bone, which
squeaked when I bit into it.

Mostly I remember my mother Kiki, fawn-colored
with white markings on her mask and forehead, and her
nice smell. The way she'd look at me deep with her brown
eyes. My mouth on one of her teats, rough and bumped
out, as she gave me her milk. The warmth of her skin as I

went to sleep, lying beside her. The steady heartbeat inside her chest.

I did not know my father. Not having a father around wasn't a problem with me and, as far as I know, it didn't worry my sister. I can tell you this: as pups, we never felt unloved or alone.

How could we feel lonely, when there were so many of us in so small a space? Besides us animals, there were human children in the apartment where we lived, and a woman, too. This was my first mistress, who went by *Darcia* to other adults, and *Mama* to her kids. She kept my mother, me, and my siblings when it might have been easier to take us to the shelter or put us out on the street. I know now that she was poor, because I have seen the other side of life.

It couldn't have been easy for her. My sister and I had the energy and recklessness that went with youth, and sometimes Miss Darcia would lose her temper with us, especially when she was stressed. Once in a while she would grab me by the nape of my neck, give me a shake, and scold me some. But later she'd be petting me, saying my name real soft. "That's my Buster," and, "That's my good boy," over and over, until I closed my eyes. She was a kind woman, and she did the best she could.

We all lived together in a place that had two bedrooms, in a building that was one of many buildings that were box-shaped and made out of bricks. A black iron, spear-topped fence surrounded the complex, and the grounds were grass-patched and mostly dirt. Miss Darcia's oldest son Troy called where we lived "the Eights." It was shabby, if you want the truth. There were water bugs in the kitchens, rats out by the Dumpsters, and old cars that no longer ran, parked in the lot. But we didn't know that a nicer world existed outside that fence. We were comfortable there. We were good.

Everything was fine, until that one day, when a man came to our home in the Eights and took me away. I will talk about him later. But first, some more about those early months of my life, and the apartment complex where we stayed. A place called Capitol Gardens, deep in the southeast part of the city, in Washington, DC.

Besides Troy, who was a tall, thin young man, there were two other children: Darius, an energetic boy with big ears, and Linda, a happy little girl with a bright smile. Miss Darcia decorated Linda's braids with seashells and such. As for clothing and sneakers, Linda never went without. The two young ones in one bedroom and Miss Darcia had the other. Troy slept out on a pullout couch. Mostly the kids stayed in the living room, which held a big television set, another sofa, and a long glass table. There were usually cans of soda, bags of chips, candy wrappers, and other stuff on the table. My sister and I liked to get our noses into the bags and tear them up. When we did that, Miss Darcia raised her voice. But I could see a little smile coming up on the side of her mouth, even as she took those bags away.

Troy was in and out of the apartment quite a bit, but when he was there he played video games on the television set, sometimes with Darius. When they were not playing those games, they stared at shows and programs on the screen. I'm saying, the television was always on in that apartment. I didn't watch it directly because the light hurt my eyes. But listening to the sounds coming from the TV set is partly how I learned human language. And I listened real close to the words spoken by Miss Darcia and her kids.

Above the television set was something like a blanket hung on the wall. It was made of black velvet and there was a picture of a large brown animal, also velvet, stitched upon it. I used to stare at that animal and admire it. It was tall and muscular, and it had hair coming off its head and flowing around its neck. One time, Troy saw me staring, chuckled some, and said, "Buster thinks that's a big old dog. Guess he never seen a horse." I *had* seen horses on the television, a bunch of them in fact, running around a dirt track. I just admired that picture, was all it was.

At first, my world was that living room. My mother had a bed, a green round stuffed thing that was soft and stayed on the floor, right next to the kitchen. I kept my squeeze toy beside the bed. My mother fed us, and as we got older, Miss Darcia took on that task. She poured cool water into a shiny metal bowl that I lapped up with my tongue. Made sure we had dry food in another bowl, and sometimes scraps from the table where the kids ate. I was old enough to chew by then. Kiki had stopped giving me her milk as I got bigger. I guess she was telling me, *You are growing up.*

By that time, my brothers and sisters had begun to disappear. I don't know where they went, but I have a vague recollection of Troy handing one of my brothers to a friend of his who was often hanging around. I didn't like this boy, though he never did me any wrong. He looked plain mean, and he said words that made Miss Darcia frown. Troy told him, "Watch your mouth in front of my mother." The boy just smiled in his slick way. But anyway, he took my last brother. That left Sandy, me, and my mom. The three of us there, living with Miss Darcia and her kids. This is where my memories begin to get clear.

When the weather was nice, Miss Darcia would take

us outside. Our mother would come with us, too. At the back of the apartment building there was a metal pole with metal arms on which Miss Darcia hung wet clothing and bed stuff she had washed. The whole thing could be turned so the clothes and sheets would catch the moving sun. Out there, Sandy and I played tug-of-war with a toy that had mouth handles on both ends of it. My mother watched us and Miss Darcia sat in a white plastic chair. As we played, the two of us growled and laughed at each other with our eyes. If I fell down, I recovered quickly. I was losing that clumsiness I had when I was a young pup.

When someone we didn't know, kid or adult, walked toward us, my mother would stand and get in front of us until that person passed. Miss Darcia would smile and say, "That's right, Kiki, you protect your children." I felt safe out there with my mom.

On those spring days, we would get a rare glimpse of our small community. There were more women than men, and a whole lot of kids. Some of the men who left each morning wore ties. The people who lived around us had skin in shades of brown and almost black. Most were in the middle, color-wise, but some were light and some were dark. When White people came around, which was not often, I noticed that they had different skin tones, too.

In the parking lot, young people gathered around the

cars, and you could hear music coming from inside them, drumbeats and a mixture of talking and singing. I recognized this kind of music, since it was what Troy listened to when he was in the apartment.

Some of the young men in the lot owned dogs with thick necks, big heads, and trap-like jaws. I would later come to know these dogs as pit bull terriers. They were not evil but they had been bred and trained to fight, and were naturally equipped to prevail. Pits could be fierce. I would see other dogs lie down on their backs and show their necks to these dogs, which was their way of telling the pit bulls that they would never think to rise up against them. When I saw that, I told myself that I would never act that way to another dog. Even then, I was prideful in that way.

On the grounds of the complex, there was a playground for children, with bars and stuff for them to climb and hang from, but it didn't get much use, because it was rusty. Miss Darcia warned Darius and Linda not to play on that "broke jungle gym," and they obeyed. Matter of fact, I never did see any kids using it. Teenagers kind of took that area over, and smoked there at night.

Sometimes, on those outside days, Darius and his young friends would play with us too rough. I had that toy with one of the handles in my mouth once, and Darius grabbed the other end of it and twirled me around. I wasn't about to let go of it, even as I got dizzy and my neck got to hurting. I was stubborn like that. I must have yelped or something, because Miss Darcia screamed at Darius to stop and the sound made his friends run away. Darius didn't mean to hurt me, I knew. Like me, he was just a boy, looking to have fun. He must have felt bad, though, 'cause that night he held me in his lap while he watched TV. He smelled like sweat and the sour candy he liked.

Those were happy days. The only time I'd get stressed was when I was hungry. I expected to be fed a certain time each day. Dogs come to feel when feeding time nears. Sometimes Miss Darcia would forget, what with everything else she had going on, so I'd cry and whine. "Don't be impatient, Buster," she say. "You know I always fill your dish." That was true.

Every so often, Miss Darcia would have a visitor over to the apartment, an older man she called James. James came by to fix things, but we could all tell that this was just an excuse for him and Miss Darcia to meet. She would wear nicer clothes and paint her eyes and lips when James was coming around, and sometimes he didn't do much more than screw in a light bulb on his visits. Miss Darcia was not what I'd call pretty, yet the goodness inside her showed on her face. James could look nice, too.

He wore creased slacks and a shirt unbuttoned to show a gold medallion lying flat on his brown chest. There was grease under his fingernails from his job at a place where he worked on cars, but still, he looked good.

I remember this one night when the two of them were at the kitchen table, drinking wine from juice glasses. As the wine in the bottle went down, they laughed easily and their voices grew louder. James smoked cigarettes, and the smoke from his latest hung in the air. I was on my belly, near my mother, who was sprawled out on her green bed. Sandy was chewing on a tennis ball, and Troy and Darius were sitting on the couch, playing a video game. Linda was probably in her bedroom, talking to her dolls.

"This place is getting crowded," said James. "People and animals alike."

"I know it," said Miss Darcia. "It started when Troy brought Kiki home. She was only one dog then."

"I ain't know she was pregnant," said Troy, not turning his head, concentrating on the game on the TV screen.

"Where you get her at?" said James.

"Won her in a dice game," said Troy. "Boy couldn't back up his bet. He tried to give me an Authentic jersey he was wearing, but I didn't want that raggedy old thing. Only thing he had that I *did* want was his animal."

"He gave up that girl on a bad dice roll?"

"He didn't give her up easy," said Troy. "I had to do a little convincing, y'know what I'm saying?"

"He must not have liked that."

"So?" said Troy, in a real cocky way. He had been talking like this lately, and Miss Darcia did not like it one bit. They argued about his friends, why he was not doing well at school, and when he would get a job. He was a good young man, basically, but he was heading down the wrong road.

"It's not smart to have people hating on you out there," said James. "It might come back on you."

James said that in a way that was meant to school Troy. But Troy just shrugged. As for me, I knew my ears were up. I was learning about my mother's history, and mine, for the first time.

"That's one pretty boxer," said James. "Purebred, too. I mean, she's a real nice specimen."

"Her kids are just like her," said Troy. "Look at their markings, man."

"Yeah, they got good back and legs. They gonna be strong. Father must have been all boxer, right?"

"Prob'ly," said Troy.

"I wish I could keep 'em," said Miss Darcia, and I felt my heart kinda sink in my chest. "I managed to give the others away, but these two . . ."

"You don't have the room," said James. "Anyway, those kind of animals, big as they're gonna get, they need room to run. You're not doing those puppies any favors, keeping them in this apartment."

"Dog food's expensive," said Miss Darcia, talking herself into it.

"They past old enough," said James. "You better do it before you get too attached."

My mother's head turned in my direction. I got up and walked over to where she was. I laid myself down against her so I could feel her heart. She pressed her warm, wet muzzle into my side, almost like she was pushing me away. I believe she was telling me, gently, *It's almost time.*

I was a boxer. It was the first time anyone had said it. It made me feel proud to know that I would look like my mother someday, strong and fine. But I was also thinking about the other thing that had been said. I did not want to leave my home.

Usually, when I slept, my mother and sister were in my dreams. We would be out back of the apartment, playing with that two-handled toy, or chasing birds and squirrels. And always my mother was watching us. But in my dream that night, I was all alone.

There were no White residents living at Capitol Gardens,

though we saw a few around the apartments from time to time. No matter the color, we could always tell when a stranger was in our midst. You knew because they wore uniforms or carried clipboards, or wore name tags, and also by the way they carried themselves, aware of where they were and trying to act as if they were not. They came to the apartments to do plumbing and electrical work, or read meters, or collect money for overdue bills. When these outsiders wore guns on their sides Troy described them as "the law."

Late in the spring, with the days grown longer and warmer, a man in a uniform who was not police came to our apartment.

Sandy and I trotted to the front door soon as we heard the buzzer, Miss Darcia not far behind us. She looked through a little hole like she always did and then opened the door. A White man with rough, pinkish skin, not as tall as Troy, stood in the frame. He wore a uniform, black with thin green stripes, and he carried a tank with a hose coming out of it and some sort of nozzle on the end of the hose.

"Morning, ma'am," he said. "I'm the exterminator, Ed Grange. From Rid-a-Pest? Someone from property management should'a called . . ."

"They did," said Miss Darcia. "Come on in."

Grange hesitated for a moment, standing on the threshold. He was looking at Sandy and me.

"Don't worry about them," said Miss Darcia. "They won't bother you."

"Oh, I know it," said Grange. He had a gravelly sound to his voice. "I was just looking at 'em. I like dogs."

Grange came inside, placed his equipment on the floor, and got down on his haunches. He smiled at me. His teeth were yellow. His smile did not go with his flat brown eyes. But I was curious and proceeded toward him cautiously to smell his outstretched fist. It had blue veins on the back of it. There were veins on his forearms, too, where he had rolled the cuffs of his shirt back. I had never been this close to a White person.

Sandy had not approached him. I have always wondered if she was smarter than me, or if she knew something that I did not.

"A male, huh," said Grange, looking underneath me, then up at Miss Darcia.

"His name is Buster," said Miss Darcia.

"That's a strong boy," said Grange, rubbing at my muzzle and beneath my chin. He gripped one of my front legs, high up where it met my chest. "A real strong boy."

Grange smelled like mints. I knew that smell, because Troy chewed gum that gave off a similar scent. But

Grange's smell was not clean like Troy's. It carried an odor of tobacco, and something else. Something that was sour, like the wine James and Miss Darcia drank. Like wine, but stronger.

I backed away without giving him a lick.

"Well, let me get to work," said Grange, standing with a grunt. He picked up his tank and hose and went toward the kitchen.

Things happened quickly after that. To this day, I do not like to think of that morning in much detail. I do believe that if I had not been so curious, if I had not walked over to smell Grange's fist, my life might have turned out different.

Sometime while Grange was working, spraying stuff around the apartment to kill the roaches we had, Miss Darcia got in an argument with Troy about him not ever making his bed. Troy didn't like it. He said he didn't appreciate her treating him like a little boy when he was "a grown-ass man." After he left out the place, slamming the front door behind him, I heard Miss Darcia cry. She was still wiping tears off her face when Grange approached her in the living room. He said he was done with his work and was wondering if he could talk to her about something else.

"I'd be interested in taking one of those puppies off

your hands," said Grange. "I was just wondering if you'd consider it."

"Well . . ."

"You gotta admit, this isn't the best place for that kind of animal. He needs room to run."

"I've been thinking about letting him go," said Miss Darcia. "I can't lie."

She was stressed from her conversation with Troy. I don't believe she was thinking straight, right about then. That is why I don't blame her for what she did.

"I like that boy Buster," said Grange. "Does he have his shots? Has he been wormed?"

"I haven't done anything like that yet," said Miss Darcia. "What I mean is, I haven't got around to it."

"I can take care of it," said Grange, talking fast. "I'll get him all fixed up."

"Do you know how to care for him?"

I looked for Sandy. She had kind of pressed herself under the couch. I could see her muzzle there and nothing else. I wondered about the kids. They would stop this, talk to their mama and tell her to let me stay. But Darius was outside playing with friends, and Linda was back in her room.

"I'm a dog man," said Grange. "I've had dogs all my life. I got a big yard and a boy at home who would just love him to death."

"I don't know . . ."

I went to my bone-shaped squeeze toy. It was right by my mother's bed. My mother had not looked at me yet. I worked the toy in my mouth until it made squeaking sounds. I was desperate and afraid. I was trying to get my mother's attention, but she did not move.

"I guess it would be all right," said Miss Darcia. "Promise me you'll take care of him."

"I will, ma'am. I surely will."

"Go on, then," said Miss Darcia, turning her head away. "Love him, Mr. Grange."

Grange moved toward me. My mother had always stepped between me and harm before. But she stayed where she was. I think she must have known that this day would come.

In a quick motion, Grange bent down and scooped me up. I dropped the leopard-skin toy from my mouth. Grange got his free hand on his tank and hose, lifted it, and walked toward the door. I heard Sandy scramble out from underneath the couch and follow us. She was barking in that high-pitched way of hers. She was saying goodbye.

I wriggled out a little and managed to turn my head around Grange's arm. I looked at my mother, now looking at me. Her eyes were watery and loving and asking me for forgiveness. Her eyes were telling me to be strong.

Grange left the apartment with me under his arm. The door shut behind us with a thud.

I was shaking some, I admit. But I minded my mother and didn't cry.

TWO

GRANGE

Ed Grange had a row house in neighborhood mixed with homes like his and ones that were detached. It was run-down but a little bit nicer than where I had come from. Like all houses in DC, Grange's had an alley running behind it. I would come to know other dogs who stayed out in the fenced-in backyards. Pits, pit/lab mixes, pound dogs, shepherds, and shepherd mixes mostly. Their barks often filled the night. They were there for security.

Grange's wife was named Ruth. She was heavy in the hips, with a streak of gray in her hair like she'd been shocked. There were tattoos of birds on her forearms. She made an effort to be pleasant, though her eyes were life-less behind her smile.

Their son Teddy was very glad to meet me. There were no other children in the home and I could see in his delight that he looked at me as a potential companion and friend. His arms were very thin. He looked sick.

"Now, look," said Grange, as the three of them gathered around me, "I paid good money for this dog . . ." — that was a lie—"and you know I'm not about wastin' my money. I am going to discipline him and train him right. If it doesn't work out, it doesn't work out. I'll take him to the pound and drop him off. But we'll give it a try. See how it goes. That means all of you ha ve to pitch in. Teddy, if you want this dog, you have to promise to take care of him."

"I will," said Teddy. "What's his name?"

"Buster."

"That's going to be a big dog," said Ruth, with barely disguised dread. "Look at his paws."

"'Course he's big, he's a boxer. I *want* a big dog. But you know what it means when a dog is big?"

No one answered.

"Means he takes big shits," said Grange. "And I don't want to see any of that mess. When we let him out back, and he goes, I want that dog shit cleaned up right away. Is that clear? Teddy?"

"Yes."

"Yes, what?"

"Yes, sir."

"Take him up to your room. Get acquainted some."

Teddy snapped his fingers at me. "C'mon, Buster."

I followed Teddy up a flight of stairs. As I went along, I heard Grange and Ruth talking.

"You could have asked me before you brought that dog home," said Ruth.

"This is *my* home," said Grange. "I don't need to ask."

"Ed, you could have asked first, is all I'm saying."

"Quit talkin' and make me a drink."

I don't know how old Teddy was, because nobody ever said. He wasn't a little kid and he wasn't a teenager. He was somewhere in between. His bedroom wasn't decorated much. He had a baseball that looked new, a baseball mitt, and a small foam football sitting on a shelf, but those things were dusty and didn't seem to have gotten much use. Ruth came up that first night, dropped off an old felt blanket, and told Teddy that I could use that as my bed. She smelled like the wine Miss Darcia and James used to share in my old home. I missed that place and my mother terribly.

It was scary to be in a new house without my mother

and sister, but Teddy was kind. He talked to me that night, and showed me a book he had taken from under his bed, as if he was hiding it there. The pictures in the book were of good-looking people wearing fancy dresses and suits. Teddy told me that they were movie stars and the pictures were from "award shows" and that he was going to make clothes for people like that someday.

After a while I went to the door of his bedroom and stood there, looking back at him. He was smart enough to know I needed to pee. We went downstairs where Grange and Ruth were seated in front of a TV set, him drinking golden-colored liquor from a short glass, her drinking wine. Teddy let me out the back door and I went to the yard there, which was not really a yard in that it was concrete and mostly dirt. I relieved myself to the sounds of various dogs barking from neighboring fenced-in yards. I would come to spend a lot of time here in this yard.

Back in the house, Ruth had browned some hamburger meat in a pan. She put it in a dish beside another dish which held water. "Here you go, Buster," she said. "We'll get you some proper dog food tomorrow."

"From the old Alpo meat locker," said Grange with a chuckle, his words coming out sloppy. He added, "Hamburger's expensive."

That night, I slept on the blanket beside Teddy's bed. I

could hear the raised muffled voices of Grange and Ruth downstairs. They were arguing about something as I fell to sleep.

The next day, Grange bought a leash and what he called a choke collar, along with a big bag of dry food and some nugget-sized treats. He commenced to take me for a walk in the neighborhood. Teddy came along.

I had been walked by Troy and sometimes Miss Darcia back in the Eights. I knew how to walk on a leash. Troy had taught me in his firm but gentle way. I'd worn a collar with drawings of bones on it, but Grange threw it away. He put the choke collar on my neck and told Teddy, "Watch me."

As we walked, Grange yanked on the leash, and the collar's prongs bit into my neck. Not enough to cut it but enough to make me uncomfortable. If I pulled on the leash, Grange would yank me back hard.

"Doesn't it hurt him?" said Teddy.

"No," said Grange. "Just gets his attention, is all."

When Grange came to a stop he would pull me beside him, press down on my rump until I sat, and say, "Heel." Then he'd reach into his pocket and give me a treat. After a couple of days of that kind of repetition, I began to stop and sit beside him upon his command. I had figured it out on the first day, but I was stubborn. I didn't want to please Grange.

"See?" said Grange. "That's how you train a dog."

"Buster is smart," said Teddy.

"*I'm* smart," said Grange. "*He's* just a stupid animal. If he doesn't do what I want him to do, I punish him. If he does, I reward him. It's pretty simple."

At night, I slept in Teddy's room on the felt blanket. When Teddy was downstairs with his parents, doing his homework or watching TV, I lay at his feet or at the feet of Ruth. Grange would drink liquor at night and then move over to beer in cans. As the night wore on, his manner would change from grumpy to combative and his face would get ugly. Ruth drank wine and by the end of the night they'd argue until he'd overpower her with his raised voice. But it didn't matter what time of night it was or even if Grange was in a good mood. I obeyed his commands, yet I never sat beside him or lay at his feet. Grange thought he was my master but he was not.

He took me to an animal doctor. The office was in a small freestanding building and in the lobby there were several dogs on leashes and some cats in carriers. Many of the dogs were barking and a few of them looked anxious and scared. Grange kept me tight against him as I waited my turn.

The doctor was a woman wearing black-framed eyeglasses. Though her face looked young and unlined, she had gray hair, pulled back. She asked Grange questions and when it seemed like he wasn't understanding them, she spoke slowly, as if speaking to child.

"Has he been vaccinated at all?" said the doctor.

"I don't think he's had any shots," said Grange.

"You don't have any papers on him? No records?"

"I bought him from a Black lady in the projects," said Grange, as if that explained his own negligence.

The doctor looked at him dubiously. "Okay, we'll give him the necessary shots. Rabies and distemper. I can also neuter him today."

"What does that mean? What're you going to do to him, exactly?"

"I'll remove his testicles and the attendant structures."

"Ouch," said Grange, with short laugh.

The doctor didn't smile. "The pain is minimal."

"What's that gonna cost me?"

The doctor told him.

"Phew," said Grange. He shook his head. "I'll wait on that for now. I was thinkin' I'd make a little money off this boy and stud him."

"You don't have his papers. You don't even know if he's purebred."

"I got eyes. He's a boxer."

The doctor exhaled slowly. "He's about nine months old. That's on the tail end of when you should neuter a dog. You're going to see his behavior will be erratic. A male will get agitated if he can't . . . I'm saying, he can smell a female in heat from a mile away. Chances are he's not purebred, and chances are even greater that he'll not mate with a purebred boxer. So what you'll get is more unwanted dogs who will just end up in a pound somewhere, maybe to be euthanized. It will be much better for you and this animal if you fix him."

"I'll wait," said Grange.

It was about the money with him, always. I didn't know what all of the doctor's words meant, but I had begun to feel funny inside as of late, like I would burst if I didn't do . . . something. When the doctor said I could smell a female, she was right. Often in the backyard I'd get that feeling, thinking about the other dogs in the neighboring yards. I just knew a dog was waiting for me. I knew.

Grange went to work most days and Teddy went to school. That left me with Ruth, who was not unkind to me but not affectionate. She had never wanted me in the house and I guess she resented my presence. But she seemed to recognize that I had become an important part of Teddy's life, and she loved that boy. So she tolerated me. Also, she was the one who fed me, which made me loyal to her.

The weather had turned nicer and Ruth let me out into the yard, which I preferred to the interior of the house. Outside I could smell other dogs and watch the birds go from tree to tree. There was a nest of robin chicks on the sill of the kitchen window. The mother took care of them until they flew away.

I was getting bigger and stronger. I could *feel* my size. Others could, too. Sometimes a human would walk down the alley and back away from the fence when he or she saw me. It made me feel proud and bold.

My size and build were threatening to Grange, too. I often caught him staring at me with a wary eye.

One night Teddy painted my face with lipstick that he kept in a drawer under his clothing. I let him because it made him happy. We came downstairs. Teddy wanted to show Ruth. Ruth and Grange had been drinking as usual, and when Grange had a look at me, it angered him.

"You think that's funny, Teddy?" he said. "You like playing with makeup?"

"Ed," said Ruth, "leave him alone. He's just having fun."

"I'm not about to raise no sissy."

"You bastard," said Ruth, and she tried to slap him in the face. He caught her hand and twisted it at the wrist.

I growled at Grange and bared my teeth. It was not something I had planned.

"You dare," said Grange, to me. "You *dare.*"

He released Ruth, went into the kitchen, and came out with a broom, which he had flipped so that the bristles were pointed up. He backed me up into a corner and beat me about the hind legs and body with the broom's wood handle. It hurt me but I didn't yelp or whine.

"Stupid fuckin' animal," said Grange. "That'll teach you to rise up to me. Next time you bare your teeth at me, I'll take you to the pound and leave you there. You'll live in a cage. One of those kill shelters. Think you'll like that? Huh?"

I hightailed it up the stairs. Teddy had already gone to his room and I found him there, crying. He was lying on the floor by my blanket. I went to him and pressed my body against his.

From day one, it was never good for me in the Grange home, and the situation grew particularly grim after that night. One morning, out in the backyard, without thinking it through, I tried to jump the fence, hoping to make an escape. I couldn't quite get over the top, and Grange came out the back door in a fury and grabbed me by my choke collar. He took me into the house and beat me a couple of times with the broom handle. As I walked away, he told Ruth he was headed to the hardware store.

He returned with a length of thick chain and an iron stake. From there on out, when I was in the backyard, I would be chained to that stake. Grange instructed Ruth to keep me on it, even while he was at work, and told her that there would be "hell to pay" if she did not comply. I didn't let it humble me. When I was on the chain, I trotted back and forth and wore a track in the yard. The exercise made me strong.

Then there was a ferocious argument one night. Teddy had talked back to Grange, and Grange, his face twisted and ugly, struck Teddy in the chest with a closed fist. Teddy fell to the ground. Ruth did not physically retaliate but she screamed at Grange until the veins stood out on her neck. She said that she and her son were leaving, that she was going to stay with her mother. It chastened Grange somewhat and he followed her around and tried to talk her out of it as she gathered some things for her and Teddy. I don't think Grange believed she would do it. But she did do it. Teddy kissed me on the top of my head before they left. I never saw either of them again.

* * *

I guess Grange lost his job shortly thereafter because he was home all the time. Drinking liquor and beer.

In the daytime, he kept me out in the yard. It was now summer, and hot. There was no shade, except for under the back steps, and on the chain I couldn't reach it. So I was often out in the sun without relief. Grange left water in a bowl, but when he was drunk he sometimes forgot to refill it. A cat or a rodent had died in the alley, and as it rotted, the putrid smell of death was in the air.

An old lady who lived in a house across the alley came to the fence on a sweltering day when I was burning up and thirsty. She looked at me with pity and said, "What's that man doing to you? Don't worry, boy, I'm gonna call someone."

A sturdy man in a blue uniform came by that same day. He got out of a white van, looked me and my situation over, and shook his head. Grange must have seen him because he came out the back door, looking awful. He had lost his wife, his kid, and his job, and that combined with the drinking had aged him. I almost felt sorry for him. Almost.

"Can I help you?"

"My name is Adam, sir. I'm a Humane Society enforcement officer. We had a call that this dog was left outside without shade or water. That seems to be the case."

"You're, like, dog police?" Grange chuckled.

Adam didn't smile. "You can't keep an animal chained up in the hot sun," he said.

"He gets water."

"There's none in that dish."

"Maybe he drank it. I'll get him some."

Adam stepped forward. "Under the DC criminal code, what I'm seeing here today constitutes cruelty. Section Twenty-Two, One Thousand and One. You can look it up online. This would not be a misdemeanor charge. In the District it's a felony, punishable by a fine and up to 180 days incarceration."

"What the hell. You threatening me?"

"I'm just informing you of the law and giving you a heads-up today. I'll be back to check up on . . . what's this dog's name?"

"Buster."

"I'll be back to check up on Buster. You can't keep him on a chain or out in the sun in this heat. His water dish has to be refreshed. All the time."

"Who called you?" said Grange.

"I'll be back," said Adam. "Have a good day." He walked to his van and drove out of the alley.

Grange was muttering under his breath as he took me off the chain and told me to get into the house.

* * *

Adam returned in his white van a few days later. He saw that I was chained once again and that there was no water in my dish. Also, there was my waste, attracting flies, in piles all over the yard. Grange rarely picked it up anymore. I hadn't seen him since he put me out that morning. It wasn't unusual for him to sleep off his condition in the daytime.

Adam made a call on his phone and soon a police car arrived. Two uniformed officers got out and spoke briefly to Adam, and at the end of the conversation, Adam said, "I'm taking him."

Adam jumped over the fence, barely brushing it with his hand. He approached me correctly, his hands at his side. I opened my mouth and let my ears relax, telling him it was all right. He made a fist and let me smell it. Then he scratched me under my chin.

Adam unhooked the chain from my collar and picked me up, cradling me in his arms. "All right, Buster, let's go."

He put me in the back of his van. He gave me water and some dry food. There were windows in the rear of the van, but I didn't look back at the Grange house. I often wonder what happened to Teddy. He was nice.

We drove for a while. We were on a busy street. Through the rear windows I saw two tall towers and a parking lot filled with police cars. I didn't know where we were going exactly, but I began to think about what Grange had said to me when he threatened to drop me off at the pound. Living in a cage. Kill shelter. I began to shake.

Adam stopped the van in an alley behind a row of buildings that looked like stores and restaurants. He opened the back door and reached for my collar. I had already decided what I was going to do. I rushed past him, bumping him hard and knocking him to the side. I jumped out of the van and my legs were moving before I hit the pavement. I heard Adam yell, "Hey!" But in my head I was gone and no one could catch me. My blood was spiked.

I will never forget Adam's kindness. He saved me. But I was not going to live in a cage.

THREE

UNCLE JOE

I was on the street for a few days, on my own. There was a small forest beside a school for little kids and that's where I stayed during the day. At night I went out in the neighborhood in search of food. I found it in garbage cans and after I ate it I usually felt sick. I'd throw up and my feces were like liquid when they came out. As for water, I'd get it in bird feeders and in buckets that people left out upturned. That made me sick, too. But I was alive.

There was another dog, a mix, off its leash. I don't know if it was lost or had escaped its owner. It had wandered into the woods. I smelled that it was a female and I got swole. After a quick sniff I mounted her, holding her fast with my front legs. When I busted it was like nothing I'd ever felt. At that moment, there was no unhappiness in the world. I was still dripping as the dog scurried away. I knew then that I was full grown.

It got old staying in the woods and scrounging for food and water at night. So I went out in the day. People who had dogs on leashes walked quickly in the opposite direction when they saw me. Some of those people cursed at me. I was in a neighborhood of homes. No apartments that I could see. Those tall towers that I had noticed in Adam's van were visible, looming over the landscape. It was another hot day and I was thirsty and tired.

I came upon a dark-skinned man working on a long automobile that was parked in the shade of a portable carport in his backyard. He was kind of big around the middle and he had big hands. His kinky hair was gray on the sides and he was bald on top. His movements were slow. He reminded me of Miss Darcia's friend James, who I had liked. I stood on the edge of his yard and waited for him to notice me.

"Hey," said the man. I would later learn, through his nephew, that his name was Uncle Joe. "What're you doing there, boy?"

I walked to him and smelled his outstretched fist. He

rubbed my neck. He read my name off the tag that hung from my choke collar.

"Buster," said Uncle Joe. "Hmph."

I was panting.

"I know. You're thirsty."

Uncle Joe went through the back door of his house. He didn't tell me to stay there or wait, but I did. When he came back outside, he had a bowl of water in one hand and in the other a dish of dry food. He put them down in the shade of the carport. I ate every last bit of food and drank all the water. Then I lay down right there while he worked on his car and I went to sleep.

When Uncle Joe woke me up it was late in the day. The light was fading and shadows were long in the yard.

"Come on, Buster," said Uncle Joe. "Come inside."

I followed him into his house. There was a small, very old dog in the living room, lying on a bed cushion. She was black and her coat was flecked with gray. Her face was nearly all gray. Her eyes were black and watery.

"That's Lucy," said Uncle Joe. "Lucy, meet Buster."

I went over to Lucy and sniffed her butt. Lucy barely raised her head. Lucy didn't dislike me and she wasn't threatened. She simply wasn't interested.

"Don't mind her," said Uncle Joe. "She's just gotten old. Like me."

Uncle Joe got his phone and came over to me and read off my tag. "Ed Grange," he said. "Let me call this number and tell him I found his dog."

I started shaking. I didn't mean to.

Uncle Joe saw it and rubbed my coat. "Relax, boy. It's gonna be all right."

He called the number and hit a button on the phone so that I could hear Grange's voice. It was hard to make out the words because Grange was drunk and agitated. The last thing Grange said was, "Keep him."

I relaxed. Uncle Joe put the phone down on a table.

"Well," he said. "Looks like you'll be staying here for the night. I'm not going to call the pound. But I can't keep you, either. We'll just have to figure something out."

He *did* keep me, though. I don't know how long. But the season changed. And then it changed again. Leaves turned colors and fell off the trees, and snow dusted the ground.

Uncle Joe was a kind master, and I respected him, though there was a stillness in the house. Seemed like Uncle Joe was just waiting for something to happen. Things that were put down stayed where they were, dishes went unwashed.

One day, Uncle Joe came out of the kitchen with a

broom in hand and I ran away and hid under a bed. He found me and said, "Okay, Buster. Someone must have used a broomstick to treat you wrong. But I won't. I promise."

It was fine here, but it was not a time of discovery or excitement for me. Uncle Joe walked me twice a day, and I eagerly awaited those times, because it was then that I saw things that were new.

Lucy tolerated me. Maybe more than that. Her tail did twitch when I came over to her to say hello. She rarely got up off her bed cushion, though. And one day she stopped getting up at all. It was a couple of days like that where she just lay there and wouldn't eat.

Uncle Joe called someone. A man with a long beard came to the house, carrying a leather case. He was heavy and wore suspenders holding up blue jeans. He was so soft-spoken that when he and Uncle Joe talked I could not hear his words. Uncle Joe gave the man some money. When their business conversation was done, the man sat on the floor cross-legged beside Lucy's bed and talked to her in that same soft way. Then he reached into his bag and brought out a kit. He fixed a shot and gave Lucy an injection in her paw. She winced a little bit when the needle went in. Uncle Joe talked to her as her eyes got cloudy. He said they'd all be together soon: Uncle Joe, Lucy, and Olivia. Then the man gave her something through a flexible tube he had fitted in her leg vein. The man wrapped Lucy in a blanket and carried her out to his truck. I watched the whole thing.

Uncle Joe had been stoic during the death process, but when the man drove away, Uncle Joe began to cry. He was sitting in his favorite chair in the living room, where he watched TV. I went to him and positioned myself against his legs so he could feel my warmth.

"Lucy was Olivia's," said Uncle Joe. I guess he was talking to me, a dog, because he had to talk to someone, and I was there. "We got her from the Humane Society on Georgia Avenue. She was a puppy, just old enough to adopt. The man there put her in my arms and she fell asleep right away. On the drive home, Olivia held her and that's how Lucy got, what they call it, *imprinted* to Olivia. I was still working. This was before I retired, so it was Lucy and Olivia together all day, and Olivia fell in love with her. Our kids were out the house by then. Stands to reason that Lucy became Olivia's kid, in a way. And then, a couple years ago, Olivia passed. Lucy was what I had left of Olivia. I know it's foolish." Uncle Joe wiped a handkerchief across his face. "Anyway."

Uncle Joe threw all of Lucy's toys away and washed the cover of her bed cushion. He was very quiet for the rest of the day. That night, he made a phone call and talked to someone he addressed as *Top*.

Top Wilson came over the next day and once again my life changed.

FOUR

TOP

He was a tall young man with a good build. He was dressed nice, with fitted track pants and a clean shirt with a thin gold chain worn over it. His sneakers looked new. His hair was barbered tight and there was a small slash cut into it, like a part. What I remember most from the first time I saw Top were his eyes. Though he was physically big and strong, he didn't look like he'd use his size to hurt someone. His eyes were kind.

"You were right, Uncle Joe," said Top Wilson, looking me over, "that is one beautiful dog."

It was the first time I had heard anyone address my master by his name. We were all in Uncle Joe's living room.

"He came to me one hot day, looking tired and thirsty," said Uncle Joe. "I called his owner but he didn't want him. I couldn't bring myself to take him to the pound. He's a good dog. Hasn't been a bit of trouble."

"Why you want to get rid of him?"

My heart jumped.

"I had to put Lucy down yesterday, like I told you. I don't want to go through that again. Oh, I know, this dog could outlive me. Maybe not. But also, with my bad back, and my knees going bad on me, the truth is, I can't do this dog right. He needs a young man like you to run him and devote more time to him."

"Is he house trained?"

"Never had an accident in the house since I've had him. Doesn't pull on his leash. Good with other dogs."

"Don't you want a companion?"

"It's selfish to just keep an animal for your own self."

"Well . . ."

"You're my nephew—*grand*nephew, you want to be exact—and I know your heart. I trust you to give him a good life."

Top thought it over and nodded. "I want the option to bring him back to you, though, if it doesn't work out."

"It will. You're gonna love Buster. You'll see."

Uncle Joe talked for a while about me, what I liked

and didn't like. Our routine. He was right about every-thing. He knew me.

As Uncle Joe gathered up my leash and my rope toy, he said to Top, "You making out all right?"

"I'm good."

"You're looking prosperous."

"Business is good."

"Mind yourself," said Uncle Joe, and gave Top a long, meaningful look.

"I do," said Top. He leashed me and said to Uncle Joe, "I'll bring him by to visit. So you don't need to say good-bye."

"Take him," said Uncle Joe, and he turned his back on me and walked into the kitchen. I barked at him but he didn't respond.

We went outside to Top's car, which looked different than any car I had seen on the street. It was black with a black interior and had pretty wheels. I would later hear Top's friends call it a Monte Carlo. Top said it was "extra classic."

"That's my MC," said Top as we went around to the passenger side. He opened that door and said, "You can ride up front with me."

We drove to his spot.

* * *

Top lived in a nice new building with its own parking place on the side. His two-story apartment had an entrance on the ground floor and it was sweet. The lower level was the living area and kitchen and up a short flight of stairs was his bedroom, what Top called "my loft." There was a huge TV set mounted on a brick wall and you could step out onto a patio that had chairs and a sofa. The house backed to an alley.

Though I had been treated well by Miss Darcia and by Uncle Joe, their means were limited, and what had been given to me was nothing compared to the life given to me by Top. It wasn't just the apartment and car that told me Top was wealthy. I saw his cash. He kept it in a safe in his closet. Sometimes he'd bring it out and count it before meeting with the young men he employed. He paid them with that cash. From what I could tell, he never went outside the apartment to work. All of his business was done over his phones. He had many.

Because he didn't go out to a job, Top had time to spend with me, and we used it well. He walked me regular and took me to places that I could run off my leash. He liked a place he called the "Valley Trail," which was deep in the woods and went high above a winding creek and lasted for miles. I chased squirrels and other animals, and Top was happy. On those days, he smoked something that was not a cigarette or a cigar. It made him smile wide.

He lavished me. I had two beds, one for the living room and one for the bedroom, and toys, and delicious food, and a stainless steel water dish with my name painted on it. He installed a kind of low door within the back door that I could push on and go out of. So anytime I desired to be outside, I would go, and I didn't have to bother him. I jumped the fence to see if I could, but right away I'd jump it again and be inside the yard. I didn't want to get away.

I was as fit as I had ever been. I knew I looked good. I felt it. I was strong.

Top had a female companion, Belle, who'd come over at night. She always dressed pretty and smelled nice. She liked me, and when they were on the sofa I'd often sleep on my bed there, close to her. Late at night they'd go into Top's bedroom and he would join himself to her, sometimes from behind, the way we do. From her sounds I thought that he was hurting her, and the first time this happened I barked, which made them both laugh. I knew then from her smile and dreamy eyes that she was all right.

"Go ahead, Buster," said Top, "give us some privacy."

One night, being in that bedroom, watching them go at it, listening to her sounds, I felt myself swell. I trotted out the room and down the stairs to my back door. I went

57

through the flap and out to the backyard and jumped the fence. I stood in the alley. My nose twitched as I smelled a female dog in heat. I found her in a neighboring yard, a mix not much smaller than me. I jumped the fence where she lived, mounted the bitch, and shot a hot load inside her.

Satiated, I walked back to Top's crib, my head held high.

Top often had meetings with two men at his house. One of those meetings got a little tense.

The first guy was named Kofi and he had broad shoulders and was, for the most part, quiet. The other was a man named Ricky, who was slim and spidery, all arms and legs with a small torso. He talked too much and his cocky manner reminded me of Troy's friend, the boy who used to visit us in the Eights and would use disrespectful words in front of Miss Darcia. Kofi had intelligent eyes; Ricky's were blank. I didn't like Ricky and I guess he sensed it. He would make unasked-for suggestions to Top about how I could be a better dog.

"Why don't you cut that dog's ears so they sit up right?" said Ricky.

He meant *crop*. Troy had taken me to a doctor when he first got me and the doctor had used that word before he shortened my tail. Troy had decided to leave my ears alone.

"Ain't nothing wrong with his ears," said Top. "I like the way Buster looks."

"Saying, that dog could be correct."

"He's good right now," said Top.

The way he said it silenced the room.

"Everybody got their phones off?" said Top.

Kofi and Ricky nodded. Top had a thing about live phones. He said they could listen to conversations.

"Let's talk about the delivery," said Top. "The product is coming in from the south, in a truck. Our man Nesto is going to park the truck right on the shoulder at the spot we agreed to. You two will come up behind it in your rental van and transfer the product to the van. Give Nesto his payment. Then you drive the van to our property, unload it, and return the van to the U-Haul joint. We'll bag it up later and make the drop to our distributors."

"The way we always do," said Kofi.

"It works," said Top.

"You know," said Ricky, "that's all well and good. But I've been thinking lately, about the risk, I mean. Picking up all of that product, in bulk, hauling it all around . . . we could be taking less of a chance moving cocaine or heroin. Or any kind of pills you can name. We could make more money, too. You know?"

"I'm in the weed business," said Top. "Nobody dies behind it, nobody gets addicted. I'm selling something that makes people happy. I don't want nothing to do with that other stuff. Ever."

"Just making a suggestion."

"You made it," said Top. "I don't want to hear it again."

"You're the boss." Ricky's grin was without warmth. "Why they call you *Top*."

Ricky and Kofi got up from the couch. There was something under Ricky's shirt and Top caught it.

"One more thing, Ricky," said Top. "Don't bring a gun into my home again, hear?"

"*You* got one."

"I do. But I'm careful. You don't want to go down on a gun charge for no reason. You got a good thing going with me, right? They lock you up on a gun charge, you gonna lose a lot of money."

"Everybody got a piece," said Ricky. "I don't go nowhere without my heater. It's dangerous on these streets."

"Not in my house," said Top. "I won't tell you again."

Ricky kind of shrugged and started to walk away. He moved toward me, deliberately, expecting me, daring me, to move. But I stayed put, standing firm on my fours. Ricky kind of smiled at me then in a way that had no kindness to it. But he walked around me. He and Kofi left the place.

I walked over to Top and let him rub me under my chin. It relaxed him some. I could see that he was stressed.

Not long after that day, Top got arrested. I was riding with him in his Monte Carlo on a busy street. Top was smoking his thing and listening to his music, drums and beats, when we heard the whoop of a siren. Colored lights played around us as Top pulled over. He wetted his fingers and put out what was left of his rolled cigarette, and then he swallowed it, getting it down with a swig of water.

The police gave Top some instructions through a speaker while they stayed in their car. Top complied, rolling his window down and putting his hands high up on the steering wheel. They waited for another squad car to join them, and then four police officers approached us.

Top said, "Be still, Buster. It's gonna be all right."

The whole thing took a couple of hours. They told Top that he had "failed to make a complete stop at the four-way," and that they had "detected the odor of marijuana in the car," which gave them the right to search it. They found a gun under the seat. Top was about to get locked up for the very thing he had warned Ricky about.

As they handcuffed Top, an animal control van rolled onto the scene.

"Where you about to take him?" said Top to the nearest cop.

"City shelter," said the cop, and my stomach flipped.

Living in a cage. Kill shelter.

I began to shake. A woman who had come out of the van talked to me softly as she leashed me.

The police led Top to a squad car. Over his shoulder Top said, "I won't be a minute, Buster. I'll get you out straightaway."

A couple of the police officers laughed. I guess they thought it was funny that my master was talking to me as if I could understand. Or maybe they knew that Top would not be released as soon as he thought he would. That part of it was right.

The city shelter was on a busy stretch of a multilane road. As I had expected, I was put in a cage. It was a small room, next to and across from others, with a barred iron door. I was fed regularly and always had water, and twice a day someone took me outside to a grassy space that was enclosed by a high fence. I could run there.

The people who worked at the shelter wore blue shirts with writing on them. That's how we knew who they were.

* * *

I don't know how long I was in there. I saw many dogs come and go. Some were taken by the many people who strolled the aisles during the daylight hours, inspecting us. There were people who came with their children, and I soon deduced that young families were mainly looking for puppies.

Not all of the dogs who left the facility were adopted. The dogs who were angry and violent, those who did not respond positively to any human contact, or to other dogs, were put on a different track. I noticed that a certain colored card with writing on it was placed on the door of their cages. When a human would inquire about adopting those kinds of dogs, the people who worked in the shelter would say, "Unfortunately, we've determined that this dog is not adoptable and will be euthanized." The unadoptable dogs were taken from their cages and we never saw them again.

Knowing this, I played their game. I was friendly to anyone who stopped by my cage. I even broke my vow and allowed myself to lie on my back, paws up, and make myself appear submissive to other dogs. The workers at the shelter began to use me as a kind of test animal, to greet newcomers and determine their level of aggression. I was biding my time, hoping that Top would come for me soon.

Across the way from me at some point was a red-nosed pit bull named Trooper. Trooper was strong of flank and jaw and he held his head up. He was smart enough to not act violently to humans, but would not bow down to other dogs. We often just looked at one another from our cages. In our eyes grew respect. The workers sensed this and tried us out together, tentatively, in the run area out back. Me and Trooper played, wrestled, and tussled over ring and rope toys. I was the only dog he related to in this way. We were friends.

One afternoon, two young men came for Trooper. One of the young men wore gold chains and a diamond-studded cross outside his shirt. I could see from Trooper's positive reaction to him that this was Trooper's master. Before he took Trooper away, the shelter employee said, "Let him say goodbye to Buster," and Trooper, now leashed, came to the bars of my cage and licked my snout. I watched him walk away proudly by his master's side.

I went back to a corner and lay down, feeling sorry for myself. I wanted to be freed, too. I closed my eyes and thought of Top.

He did come for me, but before that day I was taken for a ride to another place and walked into a room where a male doctor waited. I got put up on a table and the doctor talked to me and his voice calmed me. He gave me a shot in my paw. He was still talking when I went to sleep.

When I woke up, the doctor said, "Now you can be adopted into a good home, Buster. I don't know why this wasn't done earlier, but better late than never." He put me down on the floor and I stood up and kind of stumbled the way Grange used to do when he was drinking liquor and beer. I felt woozy and something else: different.

They took me back to the shelter and put me in my cage.

More time passed and nobody adopted me. I think it was in part because Top had not cropped my ears. It made me look like a mix and not purebred, which made me less attractive as a prospect. I can thank Top for that and for many other things.

He came for me eventually. When I saw him walking toward my cage, coming down the aisle, I was so happy I peed on the floor. Top showed an employee a picture of me on his phone, and pictures of his fenced backyard, and his ID matched the information on the tags that I had come with. He signed some papers and we were gone.

Out in the Monte Carlo, Kofi was waiting. I wondered why Ricky was not there, too. I sat in the backseat as Top drove us back toward his place.

Top talked about his release and the business. Kofi was reserved and only talked when he was asked to, as was his way.

"They had me in the jail longer than I expected," said Top. "The gun charge was a parole violation from an earlier thing I had. Had to wait for my hearing to get bounced. My court date will be coming around soon, I expect." Top nodded to himself. "I got a good lawyer. He'll figure something out."

Top drove for a while without speaking. Then he looked at me in the rearview mirror. "I'm sorry, Buster. I hope you didn't suffer in there. The lady in the shelter told me they fixed you. She said it didn't hurt you." Top smiled. "Don't be upset, boy. You had your share of bitches."

By then I already knew that the doctor had taken my testicles. When I went to lick my balls, they were not there. I wasn't mad about it. It had taken the desire out of me, but not my spirit.

"Everything okay with our business?" said Top to Kofi.

"We're keeping the flow, for now. There's a boy named Maurice who's undercutting us out there, trying to move on our customers. Ricky got some ideas on how to make that right."

"I'm not interested in Ricky's ideas," said Top. "That's why I called you to come with me today. I trust *you*."

I laid myself down on the backseat and closed my eyes. I wasn't trying to listen to their conversation. I was just happy to be going home with my man.

Top was happy to be out and grateful that I had not been adopted. His girl Belle came by that first night and they got food delivered to the apartment. He set up the table nice, with candles, and they had dinner and drank something fizzy that he poured from a big bottle, and they smoked the stuff they liked to smoke that made them smile.

Afterward, they went up to Top's bedroom and I followed them. They kissed in the bed for a long time and soon their clothes came off. When he mounted her, I left them to it, and I went downstairs and got on my bed and fell asleep.

A few days later, Top drove me to a place that was in the city but felt like country, with old houses, big yards, and streets of rolling hills. Top parked and we walked into an alley where there were many people gathered around a garage. Smoke was heavy in the air and there was music coming out of a box and people were handing each other money. As we neared the crowd, I saw that two dogs were fighting in the garage. I tensed and the hair stood up on my back.

Top sensed my discomfort. "Easy, boy. I would never do you like that. Never."

Watching the fight, sitting tight against Top, I saw that one of the dogs was Trooper, my friend from the shelter. Trooper had gained purchase on the other dog, who had fallen on his back. Trooper's jaw was locked down tight on his opponent's face.

Ricky and Kofi were there. They approached Top.

"Why'd you call me?" said Top, to Ricky. "What's so important?"

Ricky nodded toward an obese man in the crowd. "I knew Maurice would be here. Wanted you to lay eyes on his fat ass, put a face on our problem. He trying to snake our customers."

"There's plenty enough for everyone," said Top.

"I don't let no one take food off my table," said Ricky.

"You're not in charge," said Top. "Saying, let him be."

Kofi and Ricky drifted. A cheer went up and some cursing as the fight ended. Trooper had been victorious. As his owner walked him back down the alley, I barked at Trooper and tried to get his attention. He looked my way but didn't seem to recognize me. His eyes were shiny and empty. There was blood on his muzzle and one of his ears was partially torn from his head.

"Come on, Buster," said Top, gently pulling on my leash. "Let's go home."

Uncle Joe came by one day. He had aged some and there was less hair on his head. He had not seen Top's apartment and Top showed him around. Uncle Joe was impressed and whistled through his teeth. Top gave him a look at the special door he had installed for me so I could go in and out the apartment on my own.

"You should put one in your own house," said Top.

"Why? Buster doesn't live with me."

"He might," said Top. "Saying, I might be going away for a while, depending on how the cards get dealt at my trial. If I do a little time, I'm hoping you'll take Buster. Only until I get out."

"Well . . ."

"Promise me, Uncle Joe. I took him off your hands when you asked me to."

"Okay, I promise. But I'm praying that you do no time."

Later, they sat in the living room, and the subject of Top's troubles came up again.

"You know," said Uncle Joe, "you might look at this arrest as an opportunity. A kind of wake-up call."

"To . . ."

"Turn your life around. Get out."

"Look at my crib, my car . . . Sure, I can go to work at a Walmart or whatnot. But how am I gonna keep all of this?"

"You won't keep it. Trust me, you don't need it. All'a these things don't matter. What's important is relationships. Family. You'll see that if you're lucky enough to live as long as I have."

Top nodded respectfully but he didn't comment or agree.

"You don't want to go to prison, do you?"

"'Course not."

"Your high-priced lawyer, I bet he could keep you out. Make some kind of deal. If you were to offer the police some kind of information, like a trade . . ."

"Give my people up?"

"Not your *own* people. Like, say, the people who you do business with."

"My connect? Nah, man, I wouldn't do that. I wouldn't."

"Just a suggestion. Understand, I'm only bringing it up because I love you, son."

"I love you, too, Uncle Joe."

If Top was stressed about getting locked up, he didn't let

it show. Matter of fact, I remember those days as our happiest. He ran me often and we took to the Valley Trail a couple times a week. The cold days ended. Green leaves had sprouted and there were yellow flowers that had come out of the ground. I chased squirrels till they scurried up the trees. I wasn't going to hurt them, and anyway, they were faster than me. To me it was a game.

My life was so good that I'd get nervous when Top left the apartment for long periods of time. I'd pace around without rest. When Top returned, he'd feel me shaking under his touch. He'd rub me under my ears and say something like, "Don't worry, boy. I have to go out for work sometimes, but I'll always come back. I'll never leave you for real. I promise." It made me feel better to hear his smooth voice and feel his touch. Eventually, I saw that his promise was genuine. He always did come back home. I learned to relax.

One evening, Top presented me with a black leather collar that had my name on it, written in diamonds. He said they were real. It didn't matter to me if it was true. The collar was beautiful and the fact that he had taken the trouble to have it made for me made me love him deep. When he put it on me, I strutted around the room.

We went for a ride that night in his Monte Carlo, the windows down because it was warm. Top rolled down a busy street where young people like him were out and having fun.

"Hey, Buster, you want to hear 'Overnight Scenario'?"

He knew I liked that song, with the drums up front and the man saying those words: *Three in the morning the pan-cake house, come on!*

I will never forget that night. The music up, me sitting beside my master up front in the passenger bucket, Top happy and smiling, both of us moving our heads to the beats. I was wearing my collar with my name on it, written in diamonds. I was a king.

The trouble started one night when Kofi and Ricky came by Top's apartment. They were excited about something. Ricky's face was beaded with sweat.

"What's wrong with you?" said Top.

"We did the thing," said Ricky.

"Tell me what this is."

"We downed Maurice."

"No," said Top. "No." He said it quietly, but I had never seen him so upset. He was struggling to keep his anger down. "Who did it?"

"I did," said Ricky, proudly. "Shot him while he was sitting in his car. No one saw it."

Kofi looked down at the floor. Top paced around the

room. After he had cooled down, he came back to face Ricky.

"Why?" said Top.

"For us. For *you*."

"I didn't ask you to," said Top. "Matter of fact, I told you not to. Didn't I." He raised his voice. "*Didn't* I."

"I made the decision, because you couldn't. Maurice was stepping on our real estate. Now it's ours again. The gun's gone. I broke it up and threw the pieces over the Douglass Bridge. No murder weapon, no witnesses. Why you stressing?"

"Get the fuck out of here," said Top. "Don't come back. I don't want you in my apartment ever again. Just . . . get out."

They left. Top sat on the couch and rubbed at his face.

Ricky called Top one night not long after their confrontation and asked him to meet somewhere so they could talk. Top had touched his phone so I could hear their conversation.

"Why tonight?"

"We need to settle our differences," said Ricky, "so we can move forward, together." Ricky gave him an address.

"Hillcrest Drive?" said Top. "That's all the way over there by Alger Park."

"You said not to come by your crib. Me and Kofi were at the McDonald's on Good Hope Road. Hillcrest is right near where we're at."

"I'm on my way," said Top. He ended the call, and to me he said, "Come on, boy."

Hillcrest Drive had some houses on one side of the road and on the other side was parkland and trees. Ricky's car, silver and new-looking, was parked along the house side of the street. Top pulled his MC behind it.

We got out and so did Ricky and Kofi. Soon as we did, a dog started barking from behind one of the houses and a spotlight came on from over its front door.

"You already woke up the neighborhood," said Top. I was beside him. Ricky and Kofi were standing together.

"We won't be long," said Ricky. "Need to put all this to rest."

"Put *what* to rest?" said Top.

"You want the long version or the short?"

"The short. We can't be standing around on this street. Those folks in that house probably called the law."

"Okay," said Ricky. "You're too soft for this business. Not everyone's cut out for it. It would be okay with me if you just retired and walked away from it. But I'm worried about you. You got a trial coming up, and you might just put down a murder for the police in exchange for a reduced sentence."

"What murder?"

"Maurice. Me."

"If you think I'd do that, you don't know me very well."

"You're making me nervous," said Ricky.

"So?" Top stepped forward. "I'm outta here. Less you planning on talking me to death. I know you don't have a gun."

"You're right, I don't," said Ricky. "Kofi does."

Kofi drew a pistol from behind his waistband and shot Top twice in the chest. The shots illuminated the street. Top fell onto his back and flopped. As he did, Kofi stood over Top and put another bullet in his head.

I growled and showed Kofi my teeth. Kofi pointed the pistol at me, then lowered it. Right about then, a police car came down Hillcrest Drive with its light bar on and no siren, followed by another rolling toward us the same way.

Kofi threw his gun toward the woods. I watched it spin and land in the grass. He meant to lose it in the forest, but it fell short of the tree line.

Kofi and Ricky got into Ricky's car and sped away. One of the squad cars, its siren now wailing, followed them and the second car stopped in the street, near where

Top lay. Two officers got out, one Black female, one White male. Their hands touched their holstered guns. I was standing off to the side in a nonthreatening way.

The White cop looked at Top but did not touch him. Top's eyes were wide open.

"This guy's dead as Tupac," he said.

I began to bark and spin in a circle. I trotted toward the woods and then back to where Top was. I barked at the Black police officer and did the same thing again. Ran toward the woods and back to Top.

"He's trying to tell us something," said the Black cop.

"Be careful," said the White cop. "You don't know what he's going to do."

The woman followed me to the edge of the woods. She had a short flashlight out and the beam of it was making a trail. I led her to the spot.

"Gun!" she shouted when she saw it.

"Don't touch it," said the White cop.

"Copy that. I'm going to stay right here so I don't lose it."

"I'll call this in," said the White cop. "And animal control."

I went back to Top and lay down in the street beside him. I cried. Soon more police arrived, along with two vans. One of them was for me.

FIVE

UNCLE JOE

I was back at the shelter, but not for long. Uncle Joe came and got me a few days later and took me back to his house.

Uncle Joe was quiet at first. He was grieving. I was, too.

"They got the boys who did it," said Uncle Joe, talking on the phone to someone. "Not that it matters. Top's gone forever, and those two will be out in what, ten or twelve years? It just . . . it don't make no sense."

Wasn't long before he stopped talking about Top. It was like I had never left Uncle Joe's house.

We settled into a pattern. Uncle Joe fed me regular

and walked me twice a day. He had installed a door for me, as Top had suggested, so I could go in and out of the house when I wanted to. I spent plenty of time in the backyard. There were birds in the trees and the yard faced the alley where I observed the neighboring dogs.

It got cold, then warmer, then hot, then cooler again as the leaves turned colors and blew off the trees. This happened many times.

"The years are passing fast now," said Uncle Joe one morning, looking out the window, not at anything in particular that I could see. I don't think he was talking to me.

Uncle Joe had put on weight since when we'd first met, but then he began to lose it. His clothes didn't fit him right anymore. He had very little hair left on top of his head, just patches of white on the sides. He stopped walking me because it became difficult for him to walk himself. I had begun to feel different too. I didn't want to run anymore.

One day Uncle Joe didn't feed me in the morning or at night. When I went to his bedroom to check on him, he was lying on the floor where he had fallen. His eyes were open the way Top's eyes had been after he was shot. I lay down beside him and went to sleep. When I woke up in the morning, Uncle Joe was still the way he was. Through the door he'd made for me, I went out into the yard. With effort I jumped the fence.

I wasn't going back to the shelter. I knew what would happen to me there. No one would want to adopt an old dog.

I trotted down the alley without looking back.

SIX

THE MILLERS

I t was a couple of days of scavenging food from trash cans and drinking rainwater from overturned lids and buckets. Something I ate or drank made me sick. The sick came out of me and I was left tired and weak. But I walked on.

I found a school for little kids in a nice neighborhood and waited until those kids had gotten on buses or were picked up by their parents. Late in the day, a few kids hung around at the school playground, either with women who didn't look like them or with women who did. I stayed back at the edge of the playground. I was not on a leash, and though I was not as fearsome-looking as I had been at one time, I was still a large dog. Some of the women took away the children they were caring for because of me.

I heard a lady say that she was going to complain or call someone. "Who would leave a dog like that unsupervised at a playground?" she said.

Ordinarily, that kind of talk would cause me to run away. Instead, I focused on one little girl who was playing alone. There was something about her that told me to stay. Nearby, on a bench, sat a woman who had blond hair like the little girl. Both of them had good eyes. They were not afraid of me. I approached the little girl, slowly, making my stump of a tail wag. The little girl put out her hand.

"Careful, Riley," said the mother. "You don't know what that dog is going to do."

I licked her hand.

"That tickles," said Riley. "See, Mom, it's nice."

I lay down and turned on my back so that Riley could rub me. As I looked at her, and she looked at me, I had a feeling about her, as if I could hear what she was saying in her mind. Right then, without saying the words out loud, she said, *You are going to be mine.*

The mother didn't fuss about me, but a little bit later she gathered up the girl and they started to walk away. I followed them, keeping well back. Riley kept turning her head to look at me and the mother redirected her and moved her along. Down at the bottom of the hill on that same street, they walked into a house that had a wide front porch and closed the door.

I took the steps up to the porch and stayed there. Dusk came, then darkness.

From time to time, Riley would come to the front window and look out, and she'd call back to her mother and father.

The street grew quiet as night settled in.

The parents, who I would come to know as Donna and Robert Miller, came out onto the porch. Robert Miller was tall and wore glasses. He held a dish of something to eat in his hand. Donna, also tall and very pretty, held a bowl of water. They put them down before me.

"So this is the magic dog that followed you home," said Robert. "Riley says it's like a fairy tale."

"He's got tags," said Donna. "He belongs to someone."

"I'll read the tags when he finishes eating," said Robert.

I ate quickly. I then held my head up so Robert could lift the tag and read it.

"Buster," said Robert. He punched the number on my tag into his phone. He talked to someone, I suppose at Uncle Joe's house. He thanked the person on the line and ended the call.

"His master died a few days ago," he said to Donna. "The woman I spoke to, a relative, said that she didn't think anyone could take care of this dog. I shouldn't even tell you this—"

"Tell me what?"

"The relative said that Buster was a sweet and loyal companion to the deceased."

"Why shouldn't you tell me?" said Donna, with a slight grin.

"Because I know you and I know where this is headed. And Riley is already head over heels."

"If we take him to the pound . . . Robert, puppies get adopted all the time. Old dogs gets euthanized."

"I know it."

"We've been talking about getting Riley a dog."

Robert looked at his wife and sighed. They shared something with their eyes and Robert kind of chuckled softly and shook his head,

"All right, Buster," he said. "Come on, boy. Come inside."

That is how I came to live with the Millers.

Robert worked in an office in the house. He typed most of the day on a laptop and sometimes talked about his "deadlines" to Donna when he was stressed or annoyed.

Donna left the house every day but was home in time to pick up Riley at her school. I guess she went to a job. When she'd leave in the morning, she was always dressed nice.

Riley was the only child in the house. She was good to me, attentive and sweet. I slept on a round cushioned bed next to her bed in a room that was painted pink. As she got older, the posters on the walls began to change. She liked to listen to music and the new posters were of people who sang and played instruments. Sometimes she'd stare at me, and I'd get that feeling again, like I was looking through a window, right into her thoughts.

The Millers were steady. They drank a little wine at night, like Miss Darcia had done, but not too much. They didn't raise their voices, and if they had an argument it was a quiet one and it never lasted long. Robert had a place where he liked to read, and on one wall shelves were filled with books. Early on, Donna grabbed a broom to sweep up some broken glass, and I yelped as I ran from the room and looked for a place to hide. After that, Donna and Robert only used a vacuum cleaner on the floors.

They took me for walks two or three times a day. At a nearby park, I'd sometimes chase a tennis ball that the Millers threw, but I'd only do it a couple of times before I lost energy and interest.

Mostly on those days in the park, I lay on my belly

in the grass and watched the birds fly from tree to tree. I had always liked to do that. I wondered how long they lived. It didn't matter, because there would always be other birds coming up to replace the ones who died, just as there would be puppies to replace the dogs who passed. The Millers would grow old and die, too, and so would Riley. All of us had to get gone to make room for the new. The birds would still fly from tree to tree and tend to their nests.

I had never been so content or comfortable as I was with the Millers. But there was a certain sameness to my days. No excitement anymore—nothing, really, to look forward to. I spent much of my time sleeping. My back legs hurt and I was tired.

The days grew hot, then cool. Leaves turned colors. Then they turned brown and fell from the trees. Snow covered the streets. Then flowers bloomed. This happened again and again. Uncle Joe had said, "The years are passing fast now." I knew now how he felt.

The Millers had bought a second bed for me in the family room where they often watched TV. Robert would make a fire there when the weather turned cold. This is where I stayed now, mostly, because it had become difficult for me to climb the stairs to Riley's room.

Riley wanted me to be comfortable. She put a leopard-print squeeze toy on my bed that was shaped like a bone. I recalled having one just like it, long ago. Once in a while, right about that time when I was drifting off to sleep, I could feel myself lying against the warm skin of my mother, though I could no longer bring the image of her up in my mind.

More clearly, at that moment between rest and sleep, I'd think of Top. What I'd see is this: Me, riding beside Top in his Monte Carlo, the windows down, the music up, both of our heads moving to the beats. My collar with my name spelled out in diamonds, my head held up, strong and proud. When Top was my master, and I was a king.

The End

Acknowledgments

Many thanks to my editor, Johnny Temple, and to Johanna Ingalls and all the good folks at Akashic Books, the innovative and principled publishing house out of Brooklyn. Much gratitude to my friend and agent Sloan Harris, who found a home for *Buster*.